# CAVEGIRL

### ABIE LONGSTAFF
### ILLUSTRATED BY SHANE CRAMPTON

BLOOMSBURY EDUCATION
LONDO

BLOOMSBURY EDUCATION
Bloomsbury Publishing Plc
50 Bedford Square, London, WC1B 3DP, UK

BLOOMSBURY, BLOOMSBURY EDUCATION and the Diana logo are
trademarks of Bloomsbury Publishing Plc

First published in Great Britain in 2019 by Bloomsbury Publishing Plc

A catalogue record for this book is available from the British Library

ISBN: PB: 978-1-4729-6276-8; ePDF: 978-1-4729-6275-1; ePub: 978-1-4729-6274-4
enhanced ePub: 978-1-4729-6958-3

2 4 6 8 10 9 7 5 3 1

Printed and bound in China by Leo Paper Products, Heshan, Guangdong

To find out more about our authors and books visit www.bloomsbury.com
and sign up for our newsletters

# Chapter One

Aggie was worried.
It was Mum's birthday tomorrow and
Aggie had no idea what to get her.
A shiny stone?
A bone needle?

A tooth dropped by a woolly mammoth?
No. Too boring.
Mum deserved something special.
Aggie's brother Dib came rushing in.

"Gron has found a piece of **amber**!" Dib said, excitedly.

"Everyone is talking about it. It's yellow and gold and it glows like the sun!"

5

"Wow!" Mum cried, "That sounds beautiful."

That's what I'll get Mum, Aggie decided. I'll ask Gron to trade it with me.

6

Aggie thought and thought.
What would Gron want?
She shivered. It was cold.
Suddenly she knew what Gron
would want.

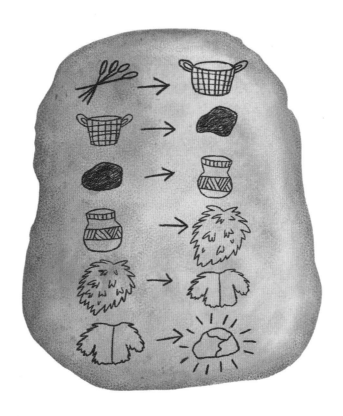

# Chapter Two

The next day, Aggie picked the strongest reeds she could find.

She spent all morning weaving them together. Her fingers grew sore and tired. But she didn't stop until she had made...

A basket!

Aggie took the basket to Urg, the fisherman.

"That's lovely," said Urg, "It would be perfect for catching trout."

"You can have it," said Aggie. "I'll swap it for some clay from the river."

Urg was an expert diver. He swam

down,

down,

down

to the river bed and
brought up a skin full of clay.
"Thank you," said Aggie.

10

# Chapter Three

Aggie mixed the clay. She added a bit of sand. She pressed it and shaped it. Before long, she had made a large pot.

"That's lovely," said Frina, the pelt trader, when she saw it. "Perfect for storing herbs."
"You can have it," said Aggie, "I'll swap it for some pelts."

Aggie put the pot in the fire pit
to harden.
Frina gave Aggie strips of pelt in
all different colours and sizes.
"Thank you," said Aggie.

Aggie spent all afternoon sewing.
She chose shiny shells for decoration.
She found soft rabbit fur for a collar.
She shaped strong bone into
buttons.

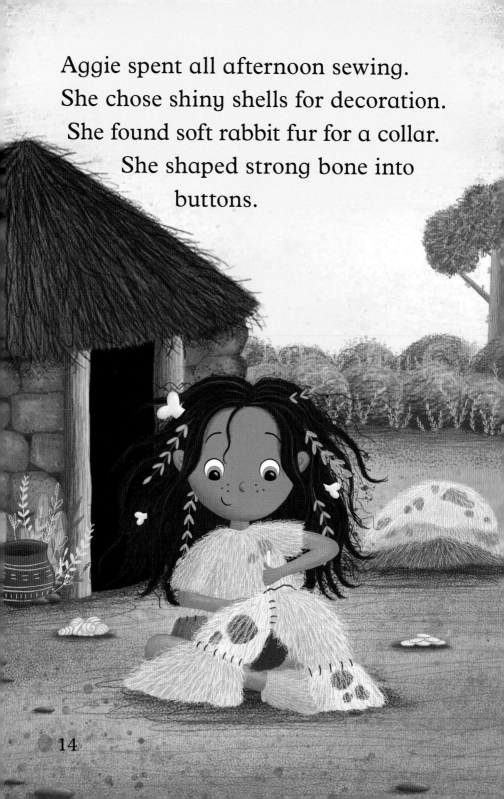

Soon she had made a coat.
The warmest, fanciest coat in the world!

I hope Gron likes this, Aggie said
to herself. I hope he thinks it's as
beautiful as his amber.
She folded it into her bag and went
to find Gron.

# Chapter Four

"I would like to trade with you," Aggie told Gron.

"The amber is very special," said Gron. "What do you have that I would want?"

17

Aggie opened her bag, and Gron gasped. The coat was magnificent! The shells shone blue and green and the collar looked warm and soft.

"It's a deal," said Gron. He shook her hand and gave her the amber. "Hooray!" cried Aggie. She held the amber up to the light. It was golden and shiny in the sun.

"Mum is going to love it!" she said.
She walked back through the trees
towards her hut, smiling as she pictured
Mum's happy face.

snuffle

scuff        scuff

snuffle

21

A large beast burst out from the bushes. It was a wild boar! A boar with hard hooves and sharp tusks. "Aaargh!" cried Aggie. She ran. Faster and faster, jumping over branches and rocks on the forest floor.

The boar thundered after her, pointing his head down, ready to strike. "Whoah!" Aggie tripped and fell. The amber flew out of her hand.

It hit the boar's head and bounced onto the ground. The boar stopped. He sniffed at the amber and...

GULP!

He swallowed it down.

"No!" cried Aggie, but the boar was gone, and so was the amber.

# Chapter Five

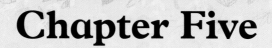

Aggie cried and cried.

She had nothing to give Mum.

Aggie kicked at stones.

She screwed up leaves.

She shouted into the trees.

A piece of bark caught her eye. It was
big and flat, pale and stiff.
She picked it up.
And then Aggie had another great idea.

She took a handful of brown dirt from the forest.
She chose a piece of charcoal from the log pile.
She found red mud by the river.
She mixed yellow clay into a paste.
She made a brush from feathers.
Then she began to paint.

# Chapter Six

That night, Aggie gave Mum her present. It was a picture of...

The basket and Urg in his canoe on the water.

The clay pot and the pelt trader with her long hair.

The beautiful coat with its shells and buttons and fur.

The amber
glowing like
the sun.

The wild boar.

"Oh Aggie, that's wonderful,"
cried Mum. "You've
made me a story."

31

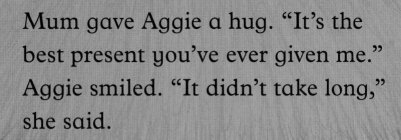

Mum gave Aggie a hug. "It's the best present you've ever given me." Aggie smiled. "It didn't take long," she said.